David and Goliath

Once upon a time, there was a man named Jesse who had three sons. They lived together happily in the mountains as shepherds. One day, the two eldest sons were called away to fight for their kingdom. The youngest was too young and small to fight, and so he stayed behind with their father.

The youngest son was named David, and he was glad to stay and tend to the family's sheep. He was a very good shepherd, and the sheep loved David too!

One day, while David was watching the sheep by himself, he heard a strange growling noise. He turned and saw a wolf coming over the edge of the hill! It looked hungry enough to eat his whole flock!

4

Thinking quickly, David made a sling and launched a rock at the wolf. The rock sailed through the air and hit the wolf on the back of the head. The wolf was so shocked that it ran away before it could steal even one little sheep! David was proud that he could defend his flock all by himself.

Some time later, as David watched the sheep in the pasture, he spotted smoke blowing over some faraway hills. He knew that the smoke meant that the fighting was coming closer.

Jesse had not seen his elder sons in a long time, and so he decided to send David to see how they were.

"Bring this bundle to your brothers," said Jesse. "And be sure to stay safe and keep far away from the fighting!"

David rode his horse through the hills, following the smoke. It was a long journey, but the sounds of the swords and the smell of food grew louder and stronger as he rode. Soon, he found himself at the camp!

In the camp, the soldiers were all running about. Everyone was in a panic!

"What's going on?" David asked a nearby soldier.

"David!" called David's older brother, "What are you doing here?"

"Hello brother," said David happily. "Father sent me with these supplies, and to see how you are. Why is everyone running about?"

Suddenly, David heard a strange booming sound.

"Follow me," said David's brother.

David's brother led him to the edge of the valley. Just beyond the soldiers' camp, there was a giant man with his own army! The giant's laughter was like thunder, and he was taller than any man David had ever seen.

"Are you all too scared to fight?" taunted the giant, his loud voice echoing through the hills. "If just one of your soldiers is brave enough to fight me, and he defeats me, my entire army will leave, or my name isn't Goliath!"

David returned to the soldiers' camp, where he found his other brother, as well as the king. They were all very frightened! No one seemed to know what to do.

"Anyone with enough courage to fight Goliath will be rewarded with many riches," promised the king.

The soldiers all looked at one another nervously, hoping someone else would take the challenge.

Seeing that all the soldiers were hesitating and nervous, David raised his hand to volunteer. He wasn't afraid!

"I will fight Goliath!" he cried.

When David stepped forward, the king looked him up and down.

"But you are so small!" said the king. "And Goliath is a giant!"

"I've been keeping my flock safe for years," said David. "I'm not scared of one mean giant!"

The king was so impressed by David's bravery that he agreed to let David fight Goliath. To keep David safe, the king gave David some of the best armor and the finest sword in the land. But the armor was far too big for little David, and he could barely lift the sword!

David thought back to how he had defended his sheep, and went to a nearby stream. There, he gathered five of the smoothest pebbles he could find. He found a leather strap in the camp for a sling, and then set off for the valley.

When Goliath saw David approaching, he began to laugh, shaking the ground beneath David's feet!

"Is this who has come to fight me?" he chuckled.

David stared up at the giant. He was so big up close that he blocked out the sun! But David was brave and not scared of the giant!

"I have come to defeat you!" he shouted.

The giant took out a sword as tall as David himself! But Goliath's large size made him slow. When he went to attack, David nimbly jumped out of the way.

David dodged about quickly, confusing Goliath. Seeing his chance, David placed one of his smooth stones in his sling and wound up.

The stone struck Goliath in the middle of his forehead. His bronze helmet let out a great *clang!*, and the giant fell to the ground. David had defeated Goliath!

True to his word, Goliath and his army retreated. David had saved the day! He, his brothers, and all the soldiers had a huge celebration! Soon, everyone throughout the land heard the story of how little David had used his smarts and bravery to defeat the giant Goliath.